The Tiny Star

The Greatest Star the World Has Ever Seen!

ARTHUR GINOLFI

Illustrated by Pat Schories

Tommy NELSON™

Thomas Nelson, Inc.

For my wife, Susan,
and my children,
Sara Anne,
Caroline Elizabeth
&
Daniel Joseph;

"Dream, believe, persist
and you will shine!"

THE TINY STAR

Text copyright © 1989, 1997 by Arthur Ginolfi.
Illustrations copyright © 1989, 1997 by Pat Schories.

The Scripture quotation noted NKJV is from The New King James Version of the Bible.
Copyright © 1979, 1980, 1982, Thomas Nelson, Inc., Publishers.

Scripture quotations are from the *International Children's Bible, New Century Version,*
copyright © 1986, 1988 by Word Publishing. Used by permission.

LIBRARY OF CONGRESS CATALOGING-IN-PUBLICATION DATA

Ginolfi, Arthur.
    The tiny star/by Arthur Ginolfi; illustrated by Pat Schories.
      p. cm.
    Summary: A special event turns a tiny, almost invisible star into one of the brightest and most beautiful stars the world has ever
seen.
    ISBN 0-8499-1510-4
    1. Jesus Christ—Nativity—Juvenile fiction. [1. Jesus Christ—Nativity—Fiction. 2. Stars—Fiction.] I. Schories, Pat, ill. II. Title.
[PZ7.G438945Ti 1997]
[E]—dc21

97-19109
CIP
AC

Printed in the United States of America
97 98 99 00 01 02 RRD 9 8 7 6 5 4 3 2 1

Arise, shine;
For your light has come!
And the glory of the Lord
is risen upon you.

ISAIAH 60:1

NKJV

A very long time ago there was a tiny star named Starlet.

She was so small she could hardly be seen.
All the other stars were much bigger and brighter
than Starlet.

At night when people looked up at the sky, they saw all the big, bright stars.

But no one ever saw Starlet.

One night Starlet asked the other stars if there was some way she could twinkle and sparkle like them. But the stars just laughed and said, "Oh, no, Starlet. You are far too small." Starlet felt very sad, and she began to cry. "No one ever sees me," she said. "I wish I were bigger."

Later that night the wise old moon looked at Starlet.

"Why are you so sad?" he asked.

"Because," said Starlet, "I try to twinkle and sparkle, but I am the smallest star in the sky, and no one ever sees me."

"Don't be sad," said the old moon gently. "How big or small you are is not important. Someday, somewhere someone will see you."

"But when?" asked Starlet.

The moon smiled and said, "Someday, somewhere." And he went on his way.

Many years passed. Night after night Starlet shone, but no one ever saw her. Then one night Starlet began to fall from the sky! Down, down, down she fell.

Starlet landed gently on the roof of a little stable.

Everything was dark and quiet. The only sounds she heard were those of the animals.

Then Starlet heard a baby crying!

Starlet looked inside the stable and saw a newborn baby lying in a manger.

"Oh!" she cried. "This stable is so cold and dark. Perhaps I can shine enough to brighten it up."

So Starlet moved closer to the baby. When the baby saw Starlet and felt the warmth of her gentle rays, he began to smile. The more the baby smiled, the brighter Starlet shone!

The whole stable glowed. It was a miracle.

As Starlet grew brighter, she began to rise. Up, up, up into the sky, higher and higher, brighter and brighter. Starlet was now the brightest star in the sky. Everyone saw the magnificent star. This was the moment she had always wished for!

And on that special night, shining over the little stable in Bethlehem, Starlet was the most beautiful star the world had ever seen.